HIDDEN
PASSAGES TO
DARK SECRETS

Books by Rebecca Hemlock

Arctic Mysteries series
Bitter Betrayal
Deadly Decisions

The Granton house series
The Secret of the 14th Room
The Secret Diary of Deadly Deception
Hidden Passages to Dark Secrets

"That the trial of your faith, being much more precious than of gold that perisheth, though it be tried with fire, might be found unto praise and honour and glory at the appearing of Jesus Christ:

1st Peter 1:7 *- (KJV)*

REBECCA HEMLOCK

HIDDEN PASSAGES TO DARK SECRETS

CHAPTER 1

Levi wasn't sure he'd ever experienced "normal." It was a word so many wished they could have. People on this earth lives their lives in so many different ways that it was nearly impossible to judge what normal is. At least that's how Levi felt. The gravel crunched as his car bounced up the Wilson driveway.

Their home sat like a fortress on the hilltop with a large barn just a few hundred yards in the distance. This place had come to feel like home to him. His heart got a little lighter each time he entered the door. It was a good reminder of what he'd spent the last year fighting for. A better life for himself and his only living relative. Living at least for now. With a flick of his wrist, Levi turned off the car and shoved the twinkling key ring into his pocket.

He was supposed to meet with Abigail, her parents, and FBI Agent Jenkins. It was as if they all thought the arrest of Delgado would be the end of this. Even Silas thought that. Levi's heart twisted in his chest remembering the pleading in his cousin's eyes that night he'd shown up, begging for Levi to help him.

"It's about time," someone call from the porch.

He looked up to see Abigail standing there with one hand resting upon her hip.

"Sorry." Levi shrugged. It was pointless to try and give her a reason for his late arrival. He'd needed some time to

10

himself, which was something she felt wasn't healthy for him.

"Everyone's waiting for you," she added. There was a slight sense of urgency to her voice. He knew why. Albert was finally going to share the information he'd sworn to protect. Information Abigail had been desperate to hear since Delgado's arrest.

Levi trotted up the porch steps, instinctively wrapping an arm around Abigail's waist. She planted a firm peck on his cheek, then guided him into the dining room. Mouthwatering scents of roasted turkey and mashed potatoes filled his nose. Albert waited at the head of the table with his elbows propping up folded hands. His wife, Nancy, looked at him from her place on her husband's left, and an open seat to Albert's right was usually where Abigail sat. Jenkins was on the other side of Nancy. Levi settled into his seat next to Abigail. The feast spread before the group made this dinner feel like Thanksgiving, but instead of thankful smiles, everyone wore sober faces. They'd each gone through so much in the last year.

"Sorry for running late," Levi muttered.

Nancy sent him a motherly understanding smile. Without any further comments, Albert bowed his head and said a blessing over the meal. Levi glanced at Abigail whose head was also bowed, then he squeezed his eyes shut. Images of Silas laying in the Intensive Care Unit of the hospital flashed before him. One could easily say that Levi's cousin was paying the piper because of his poor life choices, but didn't they pray to a merciful God?

God. Please. Silas deserves a second chance. The words didn't make sense at the same moment they went through his mind. It was God's job to decide who deserved a second chance and who didn't.

"Amen," Albert finished.

Nancy placed an enormous drumstick on Albert's plate, causing the dish to clank. The meal began silent, leaving Levi with his thoughts. He'd only lived a few decades and he'd experienced so much loss. First his parents, then Grandma, and now possibly Silas. He would be the last Corbin. Being with the Wilsons, with Abigail, gave him a glimpse of what a family was supposed to be.

From the outside, they seemed happy. Perfect even. But after getting to know them the way he had, one discovered struggles and loss in their family too. If only he could learn to deal with loss the same way Abigail had after the death of her brother, George.

"Is something wrong, Levi?" Nancy asked. Her eyebrows were raised as if her feelings were hurt. His mind raced to

13

figure out what he could've done to receive that expression from her. Then he noticed her gaze drop to his plate. Of course. He hadn't taken a single bite of the food she'd worked so hard to prepare.

Levi cut through the juicy turkey, using the side of his fork. He ran the tip of the fork through the potatoes, then took a bite of the mixture. The explosion of flavor in his mouth made him give a little hum.

"Delicious as always."

A smile returned to her face as her attention went back to her own plate, allowing silence to settle over the room once again. The silence made Levi feel more uneasy than before. This table was always full of laughter and love. He wished it was like that now. Without it, a huge aching void settled in his chest.

As everyone's plate emptied later in the meal, Albert addressed those at the table. "Have any of you ever heard of a group called the K.G.C.?"

Abigail held her fork in the air and swallowed. "They were a secret society that tried to keep the Civil War going after it ended. They were all arrested for treason or something like that."

Albert bobbed his head back and forth as if weighing his daughter's response. "Well, kind of. There have been people over the years who've tried to resurrect the K.G.C. Those people are the ones I've been protecting the gold from. To them, it's more than just gold. It's a symbol of power. Something that the Union has never been able to reclaim, and they feel that as long as it remains out of the Union's hands, there's still hope for their cause."

Albert's explanation ended abruptly, and the room once again fell silent. Levi had suspected some sort of

15

radical group behind this, but the K.G.C.? That seemed a little far-fetched.

Levi wiped his mouth with his napkin and pushed his plate aside. "You think maybe Delgado was working for someone like that or trying to start something?" He reached for his glass. Just mentioning that man's name left a sour taste in his mouth.

"I believe Delgado was trying to start something," Albert replied with a nod.

"The FBI has been on Delgado's trail for years," Jenkins started with a confused frown. "But we've never found any evidence that he was trying to start some group."

"You forget I grew up with him. Delgado's mother worked for my parents." Albert took a deep breath after his response. He sounded a bit on edge, which wasn't normal for him. His unease caused anxiety to pang Levi's stomach. He glanced at Abigail. There was a troubled expression on her face.

"How come you never told me that?" Levi asked. For a moment, he didn't feel like he knew Albert at all. The anxious storm in his stomach kicked up a notch. Why did things have to change?

Albert let out a deep breath with a frustrated huff. How could he expect Levi to know all the details if he hadn't told him?

Albert gave him the quick version of the story; it was obvious he wanted to get back to the real reason for the meeting. Apparently, Evelyn Delgado was abandoned by her husband and was forced to take any job she could to support her son, Jerry. He claimed that the Wilsons were horrible people because they fired Evelyn when they noticed some of their belongings were going missing.

"He blames me for the fact that they fell deeper into poverty after Evelyn was fired. I can't do anything to change the past and I won't apologize. My parents' actions were justified." Albert gave Levi a firm nod, as if to signal the end of his explanation.

"Was it ever proven that she took the items?" Levi fired back. He'd never heard Albert sound so calloused toward someone.

"No, but that's not important right now." Albert thumped the table with his fist. "We need to focus on the task at hand."

Nancy covered Albert's fist with her hand. "But Delgado's out of the picture now. For good this time. Can't everything just go back to normal?" Her voice had a tearful quiver to it that made Levi's heart ache once again. He hadn't considered the toll this had to be taking on her. The risk of losing her entire family was very high.

Yes, she was Abigail's mother, but she'd become a mother figure in his life as well. One he was grateful to have after losing Grandma.

"Chelsey Delgado is still out there, and she's got some connections of her own," Levi responded gently, hoping to not upset her further. He knew firsthand how dangerous Chelsey could be from his stay in the hospital. Both he and Albert nearly lost their lives that day at the hands of a Delgado.

Levi hadn't been present during the altercation between Albert Wilson and Jerry Delgado. When Abigail told him about it, she seemed dazed by it. As if it changed her father's image in her mind. A lot happened that day that would change everything. But hopefully this meeting would shed some light on it.

Abigail's gaze shot daggers at her father. "So you're saying you've been keeping tabs on Delgado all this time?" Suspicion laced her voice.

"Kind of." Her father said with a shrug. "Dorothy Corbin came to my office when I was fresh out of law school and asked me to help her with a legal matter. But it wasn't what I had imagined. I figured maybe she wanted to get a will together or something. That didn't come till much later." Albert gave a pointed look at Levi, who couldn't help but smile. The reading of the will was responsible for the beautiful woman sitting next to him. The one that now held his heart.

"I never knew that Dorothy actually knew *my* parents and had a history with the Delgado family as well," Albert continued.

Levi was just about to ask him what he meant when the table started vibrating. Jenkins picked up his phone and placed it to his ear.

"Yeah," he grunted. His eyes stared straight ahead as he listened in silence. He pressed his lips together. This had to be something important. Jenkins stood to his feet, his chair squeaking against the tile floor as his chair slid backward.

He shoved his phone in his pocket. "I need to go. There's an investigation and they need me."

"The rest can wait till you get back," Albert replied with a nod.

Jenkins returned a nod.

After the slam of the front door, Abigail leaned forward quickly. "You need to tell us everything." Frustration caused her voice to grow angrier with each word. "I don't see why he needs to be here for you to tell us all this."

Albert grunted before answering. "Because this is going to get worse before it gets better, and I want the law on our side. I don't want anything suggesting that we are the ones to blame here."

Abigail crossed her arms. "But—"

"Darling, I think we've had plenty of information to digest for one day. I agree with your father that we should have Jenkins here to avoid anyone else getting hurt." Nancy sent Levi a sympathetic glance. He knew she was referring to Silas. He'd hoped that they could have a moment of peace after everything that happened. But they did have to take into account that Chelsey Delgado had proved herself to be just as ruthless as her father and willing to help him with his cause. If they could find her and get her to lead them to the rest of Delgado's operation, Levi might just get a chance at *normal.*

*****

Levi entered the Granton House, the door squeaking as it closed behind him. He wasn't ready to go to bed. It was getting harder to live in this big empty house alone. Every evening that he crossed the threshold felt like he was

22

purposefully taking a step into quicksand. He was so tired of living alone. Hopefully he wouldn't have to for much longer—if the little black ring box sitting on his dresser worked its magic. That tiny ring— Grandma Dorothy's engagement ring— was full of family history that he hadn't shared with Abigail yet.

For a moment, he could almost smell her strawberry shampoo. It was his favorite part about kissing her forehead, the sweet fragrance wafting off her chestnut locks. Every time he smelled it, he was instantly prompted to thank the Lord for bringing her into his life.

After placing his keys on the hook next to the door, he entered the kitchen, making a beeline for the fridge to scrounge for something sweet.

Nothing.

Levi shoved the refrigerator door closed in frustration. He emptied his pockets on the counter next to the coffee pot. A few crumpled receipts, his wallet, some change. He'd half expected to be exhausted from the stress of the day. But he wasn't. Should he at least *try* to get some sleep tonight? It was probably a good idea to continue going through the books and papers spread around Grandma's room, since he wasn't going to sleep anyway.

He left the kitchen, then made his way through the living room and down the hall to Grandma's bedroom. No, his study. It wasn't her bedroom anymore. He been trying for the last six months to stop calling it that. His chest tightened. Change. So much change had occurred in the last year. A lot of it good. Some not so good. Either way, there were still so many things he was having trouble processing. Grandma Dorothy's death being one of them.

Maybe it was okay to think of it as her bedroom for a little longer. He hadn't

24

actually moved her bed out of there yet. He wasn't sure he ever would, or even wanted to. Still, he needed to go through the rest of her things. There could be more documents and artifacts he could use for the museum.

The museum. Levi released a deep sigh. The Granton Historical Society was disappointed when he told them he was postponing the museum's grand opening day. How could he even think about doing that without Silas? They were supposed to be running the museum together and Levi wasn't about to do anything against Grandma Dorothy's wishes. Especially the ones included in her will. Besides, he wasn't even ready to open yet.

He hadn't realized when he started this project that there was so much stuff that would need to be gone through. There was no shortage of interesting documents and antiques he could display in the museum. Grandma must've saved every single artifact that came into her possession.

The living room was nearly completed. He'd arranged the Victorian furniture around the room in a similar way to how it would've been in 1850s. Thank goodness there were some old photos in the house he could use as a reference for how sitting rooms were set up during those days. The bedrooms were going to be more difficult to prepare. They still had the original furniture like the living room, but also contained items that would need to be moved and stored.

He remembered how things were set up in the houses he used to give tours in back when he worked for the Columbus Ohio Historical Group. There was a designated path through the house where visitors could visit each room. Those tours took about an hour and a half due to the tour including several outbuildings.

A tour of the Granton House and the small garden, excluding his bedroom of course, would take about thirty minutes. They could get in about ten tours per day if they scheduled them just right. He didn't expect to get rich off the endeavor; he'd be happy if they made just enough to sustain the house.

Levi went to the nightstand beside Grandma's bed. It had a small drawer and shelving under it. He began pulling the stacks of papers out of the drawer and placed them next to him on the fluffy mattress. By the time he'd gotten every scrap of paper out, there was a pile about two feet tall. He sighed, thinking he'd better start a pot of coffee if he was going to get through it all tonight.

About thirty minutes later, with a half-drunk mug sitting on the nightstand, Levi hadn't even made a dent in the paper pile. Still, he kept sorting. He'd made three specific stacks that became uneven piles at the foot of the bed. One was for papers that would be used in the museum; one for important papers that Levi would box up and put in the attic for safekeeping. The last pile was for garbage. When he first started, he'd figured the garbage pile would end up being the largest. So far it was the smallest.

Humility settled over him. There was once a time he thought Grandma kept a bunch of useless junk. Turned out she knew more than he'd given her credit for. But all teenagers thought their parents knew nothing. It was a long, meticulous job, but it needed to be done. At this point, he was thankful for anything that took his mind off Silas. He'd told himself that there wasn't anything he could do for him. Still, he felt more useless with each hospital visit.

Hour after hour he read, sorted, and stacked. The clock on the wall chimed as it struck 3:00 a.m. Levi's eyes grew heavier as the bottom of the stack got closer. The letters and notes had become large, folded newspapers. Most of them were from the Granton Post, dating as far back as 1939, along with a few from Knoxville and Nashville. He unfolded the first newspaper from August 1939. The headline on the front page caused his breath to catch in his throat.

MURDER IN THE CORBIN HOUSE

Donald Abbott, a former Pinkerton detective, was murdered last night while visiting the home of the late Abel Corbin. Police say that Hattie Corbin, daughter of Abel, was staying in the house and knew the victim personally. Ms. Corbin's whereabouts are currently unknown. She has been named the prime suspect.

Levi opened the paper, spreading it out on the bed. He was just about to read the rest of the story when he saw a flash light up the bedroom windows. Levi gently slipped off the bed, making sure he didn't crumple the edges. Slowly, he moved toward the window. There shouldn't be anyone on this road at this time of night. This time of the morning, actually. He caught sight of a car parked near the front door. The car looked to be a reddish orange color, but it was hard to be sure. He mentally kicked himself for not replacing the light fixtures on the front porch sooner. A sick feeling caused his stomach to turn. He really hoped this was someone asking for directions.

Levi grabbed the .32 caliber pistol off the bookshelf near the door, praying he wouldn't have to use it. He'd never owned a gun before, but after the events of the last year, the idea of having one didn't seem so bad. He wondered for a moment if he should open the door with it in his hand. Probably not. If this was someone just asking for directions, they would think he was crazy. Maybe he should place it somewhere close by. He gently bounced the gun in his hand. It didn't weigh much at all. Something so small could cause so much damage to a person. This was all new territory for him. Territory that made him uneasy.

When he stepped into the hallway, he waited, still trying to decide how to handle the situation. There was only one option left. Tuck the pistol in the back of his pants. That was the option he went with.

As he tiptoed closer to the door, he adjusted his shirt so that the gun would be out of sight. A firm knock filled the front of the house. His body tensed. Levi took a deep breath, forcing himself to relax. Not everyone was out to get him.

C'mon, Levi. Don't be such a coward.
He felt like a child afraid of the
bogeyman.

This was probably nothing. He
pictured a friendly face, lost and confused
with a soft voice. He gave the doorknob a
squeeze before twisting it and pulling it
open. He froze. And felt the blood drain
from his face. Levi tried—and failed—to
swallow the lump in his throat. The
complete opposite of friendly stood
before him.

Chelsey Delgado pushed past Levi
and made her way into the kitchen. Two
large men—who looked like they could
twist him into a pretzel—followed her.

"Hello, Levi. Long time, no see." Her
shoulders bounced once as a broad white
smile spread across her face. Her hair was
in the same tight ponytail just like the
day he'd met her a little over a month
ago. Except now it was auburn instead of
black. Her face looked a little thicker as

well. No wonder the FBI couldn't find her. Perhaps they hadn't taken into account that she would change her appearance. She wore a black jacket that hung mid-thigh and black cotton pants.

"Get out of my house." He mumbled his response, hoping it would help keep his temper in check. How dare she just stroll in like she owned the place. She probably felt like she did with the two walls of meat at her beckon call.

"Wow, didn't your grandma teach you how to treat guests?" she chirped, strolling through the kitchen like she was on some tour. Ironic. The gun in his waistband shifted as he took another slow breath.

"This really is a beautiful kitchen." She turned toward him with a smirk. Levi knew her type. A spoiled daddy's girl who got what she wanted, when she wanted. Levi glanced at one of the bodyguards, who silently stood no more than three feet away from her. The taller of the two watched her every move. Levi couldn't help but feel sorry for the guy. She obviously wasn't afraid to use a man's emotions against him to get him to do what she wanted.

"Fine, I'll humor you. What do you want?" He grunted, crossing his arms over his chest. It may not have been a bad idea after all to bring the gun.

"I'm gonna finish what my father started. I want the gold and you're gonna give it to me." Her voice was gentle, but Levi knew it was full of venom.

"I don't know where it is. Do you know how many people have tried to find it over the years? Even if I had found it, what makes you think I would just hand it over to you?" Levi couldn't help but scoff.

The flirty demeanor vanished. Her face twisted into a frown.

"You've discovered secrets in this house. The secret room? Grant's medal of honor? All the clues are under this roof. I want the gold." She placed on hand on her tiny hip.

"Or what, your goons will beat me up?" He stuck out his thumb, pointing it toward the shorter man.

Levi's remark seemed to anger him. He charged at Levi, giving him a firm punch in the gut. His fist pushed the gun from its resting place. It fell inside Levi's pants and came out the bottom of his pant leg as he doubled over in pain. He reached for it with his right hand, his left holding his stomach, but the goon grabbed it first.

When he was able to catch his breath enough to look up from his bent position, he saw that it was now in Chelsey's hand.

"You brought that on yourself you know," she quipped.

35

Levi could feel the heat in his face. He was tired of being beaten up and pushed around. Not to mention having a gun pointed at him.

"I could kill you right now if I wanted to." She pressed her lips together, her brows raised, almost challenging him to make another move. He would have if the barrel of the gun wasn't pointed directly at his face.

"Why don't you?" he replied, clenching his jaw. He wasn't going to beg for his life if that's what she wanted.

"Because you've been going through the documents and artifacts here for months. You know what's here. That makes you valuable." She opened her jacket to reveal that she was wearing black scrubs.

"You should also know that I still work in the I.C.U. You wouldn't want Silas to take a turn for the worse." She gave him a "gotcha" wink. Levi tried to think of something to say. He wasn't afraid of her threats. He wanted to tell her that he wouldn't do it and that she was on her way to prison, but there was nothing he could say that would make this any better for him. She had him over a barrel. There was no proof that she was directly involved. She'd somehow managed to disappear the day her father was arrested. How could she still be working at the hospital right under the FBI's nose? He could tell the hospital that she was a danger to one of the patients, but he had no way of proving that either.

If he found the gold and gave it to her . . . Could he betray everyone like that? To save Silas's life. He had no choice but to agree to it. Then he would have to figure the rest out later.

"All right. It's yours." Levi wheezed, still struggling to breathe.

"You've got seventy-two hours to find it. Then the hospital will call you in

37

to say good-bye to Silas." She turned and started for the door.

"Wait just a minute. People have spent their entire lives searching for this gold. What makes you think I can find it in three days?" Levi growled.

"Not my problem, Sweetie," she said over her shoulder. Chelsey stopped right on the threshold, then turned back to face him.

"We'll be watching you. If you tell anyone about this little secret meeting or try to go to the police, Abigail will be laying right next to Silas." She gave him one last "gotcha" wink, then left, clutching his pistol in her hand. As the deadly trio disappeared out the door, the last guy slammed it behind him. Levi stood for a moment. Stunned. He should've figured they would make some kind of threat toward him if he went to the police, but they went straight for Abigail. That changed things.

CHAPTER 2

A snort caused him to jump. His eyes slowly opened. He felt the paper covered bed shift under him. Images of Chelsey and her goons flashed in his mind, reminding him that the clock was ticking on Silas's life. His face grew hot. How could he let himself fall asleep when the people closest to him were in danger?

A grunt and a stretch had him sitting up in bed. His eyes glided over every scrap of paper left at his feet. The murder article. He hadn't gotten the chance to finish reading it. He read through the first part again before gently opening the newspaper to the page that contained the rest of the story, then gave it one more skim through to make sure there were no other details he'd missed. Nothing useful. However, it made sense that a Pinkerton detective would visit Abel, especially after knowing Abel's role in the war efforts and his involvement with the Pinkertons.

The only problem here was that this article wasn't written about Abel Corbin. It was written about Hattie Corbin. Another name he'd heard before. But the groggy feeling still trapped in his head made it difficult to remember exactly when and where. His hand gently pinched the corners of the newspaper, making sure he didn't damage it. A massive ad was centered on the following page for the release of *Gone with the Wind*. Another memory of Grandma Dorothy came to the surface. It was her favorite movie. He couldn't imagine what it must've been like to experience the classic when it first released.

He turned the page again to browse through the collection of articles, scanning for any other news stories about his family. Except most of them were covered by a large piece of paper that had been placed between the pages. He pinched his eyes into a squint to read the faded writing penciled in the top corner.

To Dorothy
From Aunt Hattie
Hide this for me. Don't tell anyone.

His brow creased. That answered the question of who Hattie was. More secrets. He pulled the paper from between the newspaper pages. It was folded in half. Levi scooted off the bed, dodging the other piles of papers stacked along the edge of the floor. Excitement filled his stomach. Maybe this was it. The

key to solving this entire mystery. He let
out a sigh that was accompanied by a
growl. He was so tired of going in circles.

Once at the desk, he unfolded the
paper and let it settle on the mahogany
surface, giving it a quick swipe of his
hand to smooth it flat. Maybe he should
call Abigail. The morning sun had just
started to peek over the trees. It had to be
close to six o'clock. She'd want to be part
of anything regarding Grandma's secrets.
He didn't want to know how she would
react if he tried to wake her up this early
for anything else.

He was just about to pull his phone
from his pocket to make the call when
Chelsey's threat came to mind. The hand
going for the phone clenched into a fist. If
he didn't do exactly what Chelsey asked,
he could lose both Abigail and Silas
forever. No. He couldn't protect Abigail.
He couldn't even protect himself last
night. Turning his full attention back to

the paper before him, he gave it one more smoothing. He could see once the paper was laid out that there were small, squared creases covering the page, indicating it had been folded multiple times at one point.

The upper half was a map of the house. Similar to the one he found in one of Grandma Dorothy's books, which led him to the secret room just off the guest bedroom. The place where the Grant Medal of Honor once lay. Below the floor plan of the house, were words written in calligraphy.

My Dear Sister,

I am indebted to you for your efforts in helping us provide safe passage to these men and women. Mother and Father would be proud of you. As to your question, my answer is yes. The location of the secret door in the kitchen will suffice. The tunnel should lead into Sherman's mine. There is a barn in the woods near there where I'm told someone named Harriet Tubman will lead from there. I'm told her capabilities are beyond comparison.

> *Your loving brother,*
> *General U.S. Grant*

A warmth formed in his chest. Yet another American hero his family had been connected to.

The secret door in the kitchen. This was it. It had to be. Here was another artifact that would give everyone a better look at what these Americans went through. It is a well-known fact that Harriet Tubman was a conductor on the Underground Railroad and risked her own life to save countless others. It was a fact that Grandma made sure Levi knew growing up. He treasured her nuggets of wisdom now more than ever. His heart ached. If only he could hear them from her one more time.

There is no greater love than a man who is willing to lay down his life for his friends.

Once again . . . ironic. Chelsey may force him to do just that.

*****

After a quick shower and a hot breakfast of eggs, toast, and coffee, Levi felt fifty pounds lighter. Squeezing a steamy mug in his hand, he made his way back to Grandma's bedroom. The map was lying flat on his desk right where he'd left it. He could feel his stomach bubbling with mixed feelings. He had to be close to finding the gold. He could feel it. But finding it would only give Chelsey what she wanted. He'd lose it the moment he found it. Handing it over to her would not only save the lives of his family, but it would also betray every Corbin who'd spend their lives keeping it out of the hands of people like Chelsey.

His coffee mug found its usual place on the bookshelf next to the desk. The cool surface of the desk against his palms prompted him to take a deep breath and clear his head. His brain automatically took in the big picture at first, studying the layout as a whole. Nothing seemed out of the ordinary. It looked exactly as it did today. The next logical move was to break the picture down bit by bit. Maybe there was a tiny detail he wasn't noticing. Something that would point him in the right direction.

It was easy to see that whoever drew the map took extra care to make sure they duplicated every room perfectly. The living room, the hall, the kitchen. It felt like he was staring down into his own childhood. A lump formed in his throat when his mind drifted to memories of himself playing as his gaze went from room to room. Grandma used to tell him that childhood was precious.

Precious days are these, she'd say. This house was everything to him now, but he would tear it apart piece by piece if need be to protect his friends. His family. Levi frowned when he took another look at the lines that were meant to represent the kitchen. Something was off about it. There was a square with a hatch sketched over it located just inside the backdoor. A cellar or maybe a pantry even. Could that be it? It was the first clue he'd found in a long time and at this point, he was willing to explore the tiniest lead.

Levi pinched the corners of the map, gently lifting it off the desk. Holding it out in front of him, he made his way to the kitchen. There was only one way to see if the trapdoor was still there. The urgency in his chest transformed into excitement, even though he would have to hand over the gold the moment he found it. That was, if the gold was even down there.

He allowed the map to float down onto the kitchen table. Just as he turned toward the backdoor, a knock at the front door echoed into the kitchen. His body tensed. The pit of his stomach twisted into knots. No way Chelsey could be back; he still had two more days. A mumbled prayer that she hadn't changed her mind escaped between his lips just before his hand gripped the doorknob.

He jerked the door open ready to face Chelsey and her goons head on. But it wasn't her. Much to his surprise, Abigail stood there. Warm, moist air entered the house. Her hair was slightly damp from the misty Appalachian drizzle.

"Abby, what are you doing here?" He quickly checked every corner of his mind, making sure he wasn't forgetting any special dates or plans they'd made.

48

The slight smile she offered instantly turned into a frown.

"I came to see you. Like I do every morning before work." She held out her hand as if the memory of this was going to leap out of his forehead and into her hand. Abigail took a step forward, about to brush past him into the house. Levi took a step to the side to keep her from crossing the threshold. Her eyes grew wider. He knew that sending her away was really going to hurt her. That was something he promised he'd never do. But he didn't have a choice in this situation. This was the only way to keep her safe.

"Cut it out, Levi! I'm getting drenched out here," she snapped.

"Go to work, Abby." Levi's heartbeat quickened at the hurt he saw in her eyes. She stared back into his. A moment of silence caused the tension to increase. He had to make her understand.

"Please, stay away for a few days. I need some time." Every word he spoke seemed to make the situation worse.

"Are you mad at me? Did I do something wrong?" She held his gaze, seeming to forget about the rain. He stared at her intensely, urging her to read his mind. If only she could see inside his head, she'd know. He toyed with the idea for a few seconds to tell her about Chelsey. Maybe he could protect her. But how could he protect her if he couldn't even protect himself? He wasn't about to test Chelsey to see if she'd go through with her threats. No, the only way to protect Abigail was to keep her out of it completely.

"No, please." His voice turned into a whisper. Without another word, Abigail held up her hands and backed down the stairs. He wanted more than anything to grab her, hold her, and tell her everything. Not only was she the love of his life, but she was his best friend. She'd been there for him in ways no one else had. His insides screamed in agony as she maneuvered her car out of his driveway and disappeared from sight. Levi turned on his heel, marching like a steam engine back into the kitchen. He was going to find that gold if it was the last thing he ever did.

The back doorway was narrow. The counters were less than two feet apart. The floral linoleum would have to be peeled back. Crouching down, Levi steadied himself by resting his knees on the floor. His hand ran over that part of the floor, feeling for any indication that something had been covered up. His fingertips found a small dip. Moving along the edge of the indentions, his hand made a perfect square. Yes. This had to be the secret hatch from the drawing. No question.

He couldn't get to his feet or retrieve the tools to remove the flooring fast enough. Once the flooring was gone, the beautiful oak flooring was exposed. The outline of the trapdoor was evident now. How many times had he been in this kitchen and walked right over this?

It took a few tries with a crowbar and a grunt from Levi before a big black hole in the floor was fully exposed. He reached above his head, grabbing the flashlight from the countertop. A small part of him wanted to dive into the hole headfirst to uncover all the secrets that could be down there. The rest of him shivered at the thought of all the creepy crawlies—*and God knows what else*—living in the murky darkness. But he had no choice, so down the tiny rickety ladder he would go.

It would probably be a good idea if he had someone close by, just in case something happened. He couldn't think of a worse place to die. But there wasn't anyone he could call. He would have to do this on his own, but with a bigger, more powerful flashlight. His battery-operated lantern would be perfect and an extra battery. *You know, just in case.*

As Levi stared at the pit in front of him, he couldn't help but feel like he was being prepared for this moment his entire life. He was about to set foot in the shadowy past. Uncertain of what he would find down there, all he could do was hope it was what he'd been searching for.

CHAPTER 3

The inky black tunnel ahead of him made him question whether this was a good idea. Fear tickled the pit of his stomach. He wasn't usually afraid of the dark. Being outside at night was one thing, but the pitch blackness that the cave presented him with was a different story. There was no telling what was living down here. He inwardly kicked himself. That wasn't the thought he needed to have to get through this.

"There's no such thing as monsters." His voice echoed down the corridor. Hearing it again for the first time made him regret saying it. He wasn't five years old. He was a grown man. Levi deeply inhaled the rich, earthy scent.

C'mon, you coward. Get your act together. No, he wasn't a coward. Was he? Now he was glad that he was alone.

Levi stretched his arm in front of him, holding out the lantern. He could see some shadows ahead that indicated the tunnel was widening. Thank heaven he thought to grab his larger lantern. He could be down here having to feel his way in the dark just like the men and women running for their lives during the Civil War. That thought made him feel even more like a wimp.

Levi sensed the ground slightly descending. He scanned each section of the walls, looking for any clues that would suggest he was on the right track. The farther he went, the colder it got. He wanted to move a little faster down the long stone hallway, but he didn't want to risk missing something.

After another thirty paces, the narrow tunnel opened into a large room. He could just make out a stack of lumber in one corner and a wooden cart. In the far corner opposite of the lumber, he could see a faded light coming down another passageway. Seeing the light made it a little easier for him to breathe. The earthy smell changed to something strange. It was familiar, as if he'd smelled it a hundred times, but he couldn't put his finger on what it was. A little musty. Sulfur? No, that didn't make any sense.

Levi started in that direction. Maybe the gold wasn't down here after all. He was about halfway to the exit when he noticed several small side tunnels leading off in other directions. Abigail would love this. But could he convince her to come down here and explore them? He imagined squeezing her hand, pulling her behind him into the darkness.

He was just about to step into the cavern leading out when he noticed a black spot on the wall near the last small side passageway. Taking a few steps closer, he lifted the lantern to clearly see the splotch. The surface of the image looked as if some sort of powder had been rubbed across it. Black powder. Gun powder. Yes, he knew he recognized that smell.

Someone had used gunpowder to draw something on this wall. The pointed top with two sticks underneath. A bird of some kind. A blackbird. Or an eagle maybe. He couldn't know for sure. What he did know was that it wasn't there by accident. It had to mean something. The bright lantern showed him that the floor of this tunnel was uneven.

He placed his foot inside. The faint streaks of light pointing him toward the exit had disappeared once he was a few paces in. He made sure to take each step carefully, scanning the walls for any other markings. Another blackbird. A few steps more. A third blackbird. Three blackbirds. The Corbin Coat of Arms. Three ravens. There was no doubt now that this was what they'd been looking for.

Levi tucked his arms close to his body, rubbing his palm up and down his arm quickly to generate some heat. The small shaft opened up into a room just like the previous cave had, but this one wasn't nearly as big. The one he'd just left felt like being in a giant warehouse. This one was a tiny room. He circled the room, discovering it was a dead end.

"This doesn't make any sense," he said out loud, allowing his voice to echo down the only way out. Maybe the gold was a myth after all. Maybe it had been discovered years ago or the family had to spend it for some reason. Disappointment caught in his throat. What was he going to tell Chelsey? How was he going to save his friends?

Just as he turned to leave, the toe of his shoe bumped something. His hand went out to steady himself. Levi knelt down, wiping the dirt floor with his hand. There, under the soil was a large stone that was perfectly square.

He gave it a firm push. It didn't budge. Maybe it needed to be lifted straight up. He planted the lantern on the ground next to his boot. His fingers gripped the stone. He let out a groan as he lifted and tossed the stone away.

Under the stone lay a pit about four feet deep. There were several brown leather bags and one chest. Gold coins were scattered in the dirt around the bags The sight nearly took his breath away.

CHAPTER 4

He was determined now more than
ever to find some way to keep this out of
Chelsey's hands. Giving it to her after
everything he'd gone through—
everything Albert went through,
everything every Corbin went through for
the last one hundred and fifty years to
protect this—would be nothing less than
betrayal. He couldn't live with himself if
he went through with this. He could
figure out what to do as long as Chelsey
didn't know he'd found it.

Levi held the lantern out in front of
him. According to Grant's letter,
continuing forward would lead him out

somewhere near the barn just beyond Sherman Meadows. More than likely, Chelsey had someone watching his house to make sure he kept his mouth shut. This way, no one would know that he wasn't home, especially since his car was parked in its usual spot in front of the house. If he could make it out, he would be able to call Albert and tell him that he found it. Then, together, they could form a plan to take her out.

His breath came out in chilly puffs. His body trembled. He would have to remember to bring a jacket when he came back. The terrain steepened more and more the farther he walked. A few streams of light appeared on the wall ahead. Yes, he was almost out. The light at the end of the tunnel was in sight, urging him forward.

When he reached the end of the tunnel, he discovered that it was covered with a thicket. He wondered how close he was to the barn he'd heard so much about. Grant's letter came to mind.

Harriet Tubman will lead from there. That was why Grandma made sure he knew the important role Harriet Tubman played in the Underground Railroad. Because she was the next checkpoint heading north after the Corbin's.

Levi grabbed two handfuls of the budding brush and gave it a jerk. Not only did a piece of the plant come down, but a great deal of dirt with it. He coughed a few times, waving his hand in front of his face to take a gasp of clean air. The rest of the vines and twigs could be moved with a hard push, allowing him to climb out. He took in his surroundings. There were trees and boulders, and in the distance, Sherman Meadows. Taking a few steps forward, he turned back around toward the mine. No one could see the entrance because of the huge thicket grown over it. It made him wonder when it was in

62

operation. It seemed more of a cave than a mine. He would have to look into it more later.

Levi pulled his phone from his pocket and tapped Albert's name in his contact list. He placed the phone to his ear as it rang. No answer. Albert must be with a client or in court. That was usually the only reason his phone went to voicemail. The phone beeped after prompting Levi to leave a message.

"Albert, meet me at Sherman Meadows. You wouldn't believe me if I told you what I found. Call me back as soon as you can." He tapped the red button, hoping Albert wouldn't be too long. He didn't have much time. This way, Chelsey would have no idea that he would be getting help from Albert.

Just in case it did take a while to hear back from him, Levi decided it wouldn't hurt to take a few minutes to have a look around. Maybe there was something else here that would add to the story of Virginia Corbin and Harriet Tubman. He took a few steps and then noticed up ahead between the trees was a clear view of Sherman Meadows. He could see the fallen log with his great-great-grandfather's initials. He was just about to head off in that direction when his phone vibrated in his hand. The buzzing made him jump. Thank goodness Albert got back to him so quickly. Levi looked at the screen. It wasn't Albert at all.

A small gasp escaped his lips when he read the text message notification.

SILAS IS AWAKE. COME NOW. Using his thumb, he tapped a quick response.

ON MY WAY.

Levi couldn't get to the hospital fast enough. The time it took to rush back through Sherman's mine, up the ladder, and into his kitchen flashed by in a blur. He wasn't even sure he'd grabbed the right set of keys until he was sitting in his truck. Driving to the hospital seemed to take three times as long as it usually did.

Relief and thankfulness bubbled in his stomach when his car came to a stop in the hospital parking lot. He broke out in a run as he navigated the maze-like hallways and stepped into the elevator. He couldn't wait to tell Albert, Abigail, and Silas that he'd finally done it. He'd found the lost Confederate gold. The only problem now was to figure out how to deal with Chelsey.

A thought began to form about what could happen if Chelsey made good on her threat. He banished the thought before the picture of what life would be like without Abigail could finish painting itself. He quickened his pace when Silas's room number came into view. When he reached the doorway, the bubbly feeling solidified and sank to the pit of his stomach.

Silas's hospital bed was tilted, holding him in a sitting position. His eyes were open. He cocked his head toward Levi when he spotted him standing on the threshold. Abigail was in the corner of the room with a tall man standing next to her. Chelsey stood next to the bed, holding a syringe in her hand. She was smiling at Levi in a way that made his skin crawl.

"Hello, Levi. We've been expecting you." Her false sweetness brought rage that he had a difficult time controlling.

"Why are you here? I still have twenty-four hours." He had to grit his teeth to avoid shouting at her.

"I told you. Silas is my patient. And you actually have twenty-two hours left," she replied with a quick glance at the leather strapped watch on her wrist. Levi went to Abigail in the corner, realizing that the tall man standing close by was one of Chelsey's goons. She wasn't just working today. She was eavesdropping.

"I'd like to talk to my cousin in private, if you please." In spite of his efforts to remain calm, his voice came out forceful. Chelsey's face lost its smile. He could tell she was just about to refuse, but suddenly remembered where she was. Maybe it was better to face her here. She couldn't call the shots like she did at his house.

"Of course, Mr. Corbin," she answered, turning to leave.

"And take your muscle with you," Levi added. The man next to Abigail looked at Chelsey then at Levi. He was just about to charge at Levi when Chelsey held up her hand.

"No, no. He's fine. They aren't going anywhere." She gestured toward Abigail and Silas.

As the pair left the room, Abigail quickly embraced Levi. He could hear her sniffling.

"I'm so sorry. That's why I had to send you away this morning. I was trying to protect you," Levi blurted out, stroking her hair and mentally thanking God that she wasn't hurt.

"That guy brought me here. I went to get lunch for me and my dad. He forced me into the car." Tears streamed down her face as she gripped his shirt tightly.

"You're lucky that's all they did," Silas's weak voice chimed in from behind Levi.

He turned. Silas had his head resting on a pillow under his neck.

"You seem like you're doing all right." He gave Silas's shoulder a firm pat that caused him to grimace.

"Sorry." Levi quickly let his hand drop back to his side.

"I assume you have some sort of plan to get us out of this mess." Silas's tone was full of expectation. Levi wished he had a full proof plan that would guarantee everything would be all right. But he didn't.

"I was hoping to get Albert's help with that, but I can't get through to him." He held up his phone.

Abigail paced. "He would've called me by now to see where I was. I was due back at the office over an hour ago." The worry in her voice grew with each word.

Levi felt like his insides were ripping apart. He couldn't stand to see her cry.

"I'm sure he's fine," he said, pulling her in for another hug. "Something important must've come up." He tried to sound as convincing as he could, in spite of his own concerns. If Chelsey was picking up the mantle from her father,

69

then Albert would also be one of her targets.

"Or they've killed him," Abigail burst out.

"They are using everything they can as leverage to get their hands on the gold. I don't think they would jeopardize that at this point." Yes. That was a viable argument. It actually gave him a little peace of mind.

"Besides, I have the upper hand in this situation." Levi couldn't help but smile as the excitement of his discovery resurfaced.

"Now I know you've gone crazy." Silas rolled his eyes.

"Oh, ye of little faith . . . I found it."

CHAPTER 5

Judging from the clock on the wall, about ten minutes passed since Chelsey left the room. Levi knew they would return at any moment, taking him away to direct them to the gold. If he told them he'd found it and refused to take them to it, they'd kill Silas and Abigail. If he told them he hadn't found it yet, they'd kill Silas and Abigail. He might be able to convince them to give him more time. But Chelsey had kept her word up to this point. She could very well have them killed and threaten to kill him if he didn't find it soon. Still, he had to figure out something to tell them. At least until he

71

was able to get help. The only thing he could do right now was to get them as far away from this room as possible.

"I still can't get through to my dad." Abigail held up her phone as if the problem was with the device itself.

"We need to get ourselves out of this situation before worrying about him," Silas spoke unsympathetically. It was easy to understand why; His face was etched with fatigue and weakness.

Abigail opened her mouth to fire back at Silas but stopped when Chelsey's bodyguard re-entered the room alone. His eyes locked onto Levi. He crossed the room and stopped within inches of him. Levi tilted his head back; the guy had to be almost a whole foot taller than him.

"You ready to go show us where the gold is buried?" The hulk wannabe wore a smirk.   Levi found himself blinking quickly as his breath hit his eyes and forehead. "I guess so," he responded. It

72

was all he could think to say. He would have to take this one step at a time.

Silas groaned and pointed a finger at the hulk. "If I find out anything happened to him, I'm coming for you." The bodyguard laughed at Silas's threat.

"Bring it on, tough guy," he retorted at the same time he put his hand in the middle of Levi's back and gave him a firm shove out the door.

Levi glanced back over his shoulder. Silas remained silent but the anger was evident. There was nothing he could do. Abigail's jaw twitched. Her face was expressionless. Just before they disappeared from view, she silently mouthed, *I love you.*

His gut clenched. He didn't get to say it back. But he would. He would finish this once and for all.

Sherman Meadows was a beautiful place, but it was the last place Levi wanted to be right now. He wasn't able to appreciate its lush green grass or the smell of honeysuckle that lingered in the air. So many bad things happened here in the last few months. He'd considered coming out here to take a look at some of the names etched in the tombstones surrounding Abel Corbin, but he couldn't bring himself to make the drive.

"This is such a lovely spot." Chelsey held her arms out, taking in the field. Levi and the two bodyguards climbed out of the car, joining her. She turned to face Levi.

"You're going to lead the way. There's no reason for any stupid irrational moves. If we don't find it, you can kiss your pretty little girlfriend goodbye. And if you try to run, William will shoot you." She tilted her head to the side with a cutesy smile.

"You'd really go to prison for murder? You can still walk away from this. Do you want to end up like you father? Spending the rest of your life behind bars? You're young." Levi couldn't believe he was pleading with her. The smile she wore slowly disappeared.

"My dad was all I had. He was everything to me. Everything he did, was for me. I need to do this for him." She scoffed then laughed softly in a way that made Levi think of the Wicked Witch from *The Wizard of Oz.* "You don't understand. How could you? You never had a father."

Her last few words stabbed like a knife in the middle of his chest. He instantly regretting trying to talk some sense into her. She was determined to ruin her life and he wasn't about to stand in her way.

"Lead the way," she said, gesturing toward the meadow once again. Levi started in the direction of the cavern. A mixture churned in his stomach. Anger?

75

Sadness? Disappointment? He didn't know. What he did know was that he hated himself right now. There had to be some way out of this without them getting what they wanted. He couldn't let this happen. He couldn't let them win.

They reached the other end of the field and was entering the woods. They didn't have much farther to go before coming upon the entrance to the tunnels. His only hope now was Albert. If he'd heard the voicemail, Levi would be saved.

God, please don't let him come alone. Jenkins would be really handy to have right now.

"Are we getting close?" Chelsey asked, cutting into his thoughts.

"Almost there," Levi said over his shoulder. The thicket covering the cave came into view. His heart sank. He didn't cover it back over well enough when he went back through the tunnel to his house. He'd been so excited about Silas waking up.

"I see it!" William shrieked. They walked faster behind him, forcing him to walk faster as well. He stopped at the edge of the thicket. Williams pulled a machete from a black backpack Levi didn't realize he was wearing and began taking huge whacks at the limbs and twigs. In less than five minutes, it was as if the thicket had never existed. The trio stood for a moment, staring at the gaping hole in the hillside. Levi couldn't remember a moment in his life that he'd ever felt so defeated.

"Come along, gentlemen. This will truly be a sight to behold," Chelsey announced.

"I'm afraid it's a sight you'll never get to see," said a voice from behind them. They whipped around to see Jenkins pointing a pistol directly at them. Four other federal agents stood behind him. For once, Chelsey was speechless. She stood staring at the agents.

Levi nearly fell to the ground with relief. He backed away from his three captors, allowing the agents to surround them and slap handcuffs on them.

"You don't understand. There's gold in that cave! Confederate gold. It's mine!" she screamed. None of the agents paid attention to anything she said. Levi followed them back to Sherman Meadows. There were three black suburbans parked in front of Chelsey's SUV.

"The gold is back there! We need to get it! The Confederate gold—"

"The Confederate gold is a myth, young lady." Albert circled the SUV directly in front of Chelsey's. The sight of him caused her face to twist with rage.

"This is all your fault! My father is gone because of you!" Her face reddened, and tears filled her eyes. The agents

78

placed her into the vehicle before she could hiss another word.

"I'm glad you're all right. You had us worried when we couldn't reach you," Levi explained, following Jenkins's prompt to get into the first SUV. Albert followed.

Albert climbed in behind Levi and shut the door. "I'd just finished listening to your voicemail when Abigail called me and told me what happened. I called Jenkins and we got here as soon as we could."

Although he was still trying to process what he'd just been through, a small spark of excitement ignited in him.

"I found the—"

Albert's head shot in his direction, and he held a finger across his lips. His eyes grew wide, conveying to Levi that he should be quiet. For a moment, it was as if he could read Albert's mind. He didn't want Jenkins knowing that he'd found the gold. But why? They'd included him in everything up to this point. Levi nodded that he understood. It could wait. What really mattered was the danger was over. His family was safe. His friends were safe.

A Week Later

Levi stood on the front porch of the Wilsons' house, taking in the view of the hilltop. He inhaled a deep breath of the sweet Appalachian air. Summer was just around the corner. He knew because the hint of green onion met his nostrils.

"Mind if I join you?" Albert asked, letting the storm door close behind him. He had a steaming cup of coffee in his hand.

"Just taking a breather."

"Let's take a breather sitting down. Shall we?" Albert motioned toward the two white rocking chairs behind him. Levi followed.

Albert blew on his coffee, then took a cautious sip. "Have you decided what you're going to do with the gold?"

"You want me to decide?" Levi scratched the back of his head. "I thought you were in charge of that."

"No. I was supposed to keep it for you and Silas. I promise Dorothy I would make sure you and Silas got it if I ever found it." Albert kicked off the porch, sending his chair rocking back and forth.

"Then I'll give you half my share." It wasn't right for Albert to invest so much of his time into Levi's family for nothing. Every moment Albert's life was put at risk flashed in his mind.

"No, Levi. I don't need it. I don't want it."

"I want to do something to repay you. You've been there for me, for Silas, and you were there for my grandma . . .

81

when I wasn't." Levi could barely get out the last few words.

Albert slowed his rocking chair. "There is something you can do for me."

"What's that?"

He paused, pushed off again, and took another sip of coffee. "Dorothy said that house must always have a Corbin in it. So I'd better get some grandchildren at some point."

Levi burst out laughing. It was the last thing he'd expected his future father-in-law to say. He couldn't remember laughing like that, ever. He wasn't sure how Albert and Nancy would take the news when they found out he'd proposed to Abigail the day before.

"You got it." Levi gave Albert's hand a firm shake as if they sealed some big business deal. Albert took a sip of his coffee.

"Levi, your grandmother was devastated when your father showed no interest in learning the family history along with the clues put in place. You showing interest gave her hope until you moved away. She'd be overjoyed to know what you are doing with the house now. Did you know that you make the tenth generation of Corbins to be living in that house?"

That was a piece of information Levi had never heard before. "How do you know that?"

"Your grandmother told me," Albert answered. "It kind of reminds me of the parable that Jesus told to His disciples about the woman with the ten pieces of silver."

"In what way?" Levi asked.

"She started with ten and lost one. Then she lit a candle and searched her house for it until she found it. After that, she called her friends over to celebrate. Not only had she found her missing treasure, but in the hardest moment of searching for it, she was alone. Just like that lost coin."

Albert's point caused Levi's brow to furrow as the story he'd heard a million times before took on new meaning. "It's easy to feel lost. It's even easier to feel like your life has no value." The words slipped out of Levi's mouth before he could stop them. Albert set his coffee on the floor next to his chair, then reached across and gripped his shoulder.

"Just because the coin was lost, doesn't mean it lost its value. That gold has been in that cave for one hundred and fifty years, sitting in the darkness. Actually, it's even more valuable now.

"The dark times make us stronger. God said that when our faith is tried, it's more precious than gold. Each generation of your family may have been devoted to protecting the gold, keeping it out of the wrong hands. But God has been doing the same thing with your life."

Levi had never thought of it that way. The darkness was a tool God used. Anything can be used by God to change your life. Even the death of the person that means the most to you. Levi pressed his lips together, using every muscle in his face to hold back tears. He didn't want to cry in front of his future father-in-law.

"Thanks," Levi finally said with a smile. Albert smiled back, giving Levi a firm pat on the back.

"I can't wait to be there when that house holds the next generation of Corbins. That gold will fund your museum for the next one hundred and fifty years." Albert let out a joyful chuckle.

It made sense to Levi now, why Albert didn't want Jenkins to know that he'd found the gold. It didn't belong to the FBI. It belonged here. It belonged to the Corbin family. It belonged to the Granton House.

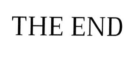

THE END

Authors Note

Thank you so much for taking these adventures with Levi. This series will always be close to my heart and will probably be my all time favorite thing I've written. I wanted Levi to reflect the rich history and culture of Appalachia that I love so much. Even though he is orphaned at a young age, he still gains knowledge of family values. Every character you've read about is written after true Appalachians (neighbors or friends of mine).

Although there are instances where I had to use my creative license in this story, most of the historical elements are true. U.S. Grant did have a sister named Virginia Corbin, and there really was an Abel Corbin related to her. I also want to point out that there is no evidence that U.S. Grant ever won the Medal of Honor. I chose this particular medal for The Secret of the 14th Room because it seems like it should exist.

The information you've read about Alan Pinkerton and the Pinkerton Detective agency is also true. Except for the part about Abel Corbin being the youngest Pinkerton Detective. I have to add that my clues about the legendary Confederate gold are fictional. Yet, some are inspired by actual "clues." There is no concrete evidence that the gold is real, but some claim that it is. I'll let you decide.

I pray that my books touch your life and help you remember that even though bad things can happen to good people,

God is still in control and can use anything to strengthen us and make us better people.

Rebecca Hemlock

Rebecca Hemlock is an Award-winning author and has written articles, books, and short stories for many years. She has worked as a freelance journalist for 4 years. She is currently a member of Sisters in Crime and American Christian Fiction Writers. Her books have also made it to the Amazon.com #1 bestseller list several times.

Aside from writing Romance and suspense, Rebecca enjoys writing children's fiction. Her first children's book, The Lost Soldier, was published in 2016 by Westbow Press. She has a total of 3 children's books, all published under the name R.C. Burch from 2016 to 2017. Rebecca has earned a degree in English and an Appalachian Studies certificate in Creative Writing. Her favorite times to write are early in the morning when the sun is coming up and at sunset. Rebecca lives in Eastern Kentucky with her husband and children.

SIGN UP FOR REBECCA'S NEWSLETTER. KEEP UP TO
DATE ON BOOK RELEASES AND EVENTS.

Rebeccahemlock.com